E
Lec

**DATE DUE**

2/10

| | | |
|---|---|---|
| MAR 0 3 2010 | | |
| APR 1 4 2010 | | |
| MAY 0 4 2010 | | |
| JUN 0 3 2010 | | |
| JUN 1 0 2010 | | |
| JUN 2 3 2010 | | |
| SEP 0 4 2010 | | |
| OCT 2 2 2010 | | |
| JUN 1 2 2015 | | |
| JUL 0 1 2016 | | |
| AUG 2 3 2016 | | |
| JUN 2 2 2018 | | |
| AUG 1 3 2019 | | |

DEMCO 38-296

For my sister Marie

First edition 2009

Library of Congress Cataloging-in-Publication Data
Lechner, John, date.
The clever stick / John M. Lechner. —1st ed.
p.   cm.
Summary: A very clever stick finally discovers how he can communicate with the world around him.
ISBN 978-0-7636-3950-1
[1. Drawing—Fiction. 2. Communication—Fiction.]   I. Title
PZ7.L4846Cl 2009
[E]—dc22      2008024230

2 4 6 8 10 9 7 5 3 1

Printed in China

This book was typeset in Journal.
The illustrations were done in ink and watercolor.

Candlewick Press
99 Dover Street
Somerville, Massachusetts 02144

visit us at www.candlewick.com

# The Clever Stick

John Lechner

CANDLEWICK PRESS

He would sit in the sand
and think up all sorts of
clever things.

He would float down the
stream, making up poetry.

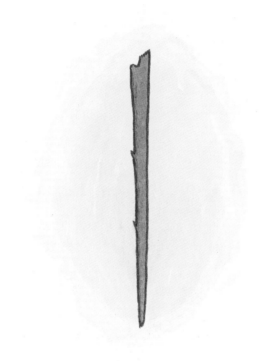

Once upon a time, there
was a clever stick.

Ever since he had
fallen off the tree,
he had been sharp.

He would listen to the singing
of the birds and wonder what
made it sound so beautiful.

When he came across a frog writing a poem, he wanted to share a simile about the sun being like a dragon.

But he could not.

And when he saw a wild rose growing in the field, he longed to tell her how beautiful she was.

But he could only remain silent.

One bright day as the stick approached
the meadow, he tried to say hello to
all the animals, insects, and flowers by
bowing deeply . . .

But the stick didn't even notice.
He drew faster and faster.

Finally, he stopped. The dust cleared . . .

but he tripped on a pebble and fell
flat on his face.

Nobody even noticed.

The clever stick
did not feel so
clever anymore.

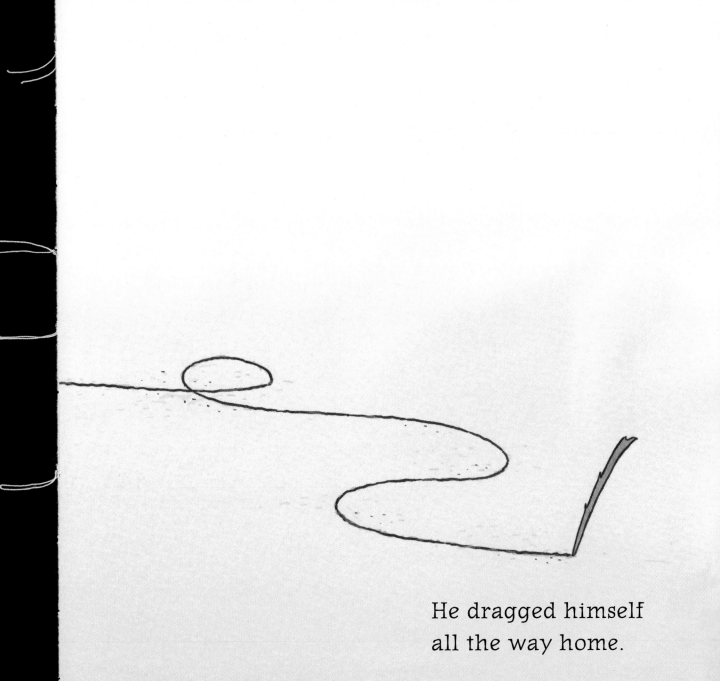

He dragged himself
all the way home.

When he finally stopped, he noticed
the trail he had left in the sand.

It looked interesting,
so he made more lines.

To his amazement, he discovered that he could draw lines to look like things.

The stick began to draw vigorously
in the sand. A giant tapestry emerged
from the dust.

As he scribbled, the plants and animals gathered around and watched in rapt attention.

and there was the most magnificent
sight the forest had ever seen.

The animals cheered, the insects buzzed, and the trees swayed their branches in approval.

Even the rose turned
her petals to look.

At that moment, a drop of water
fell from the sky . . . then another.

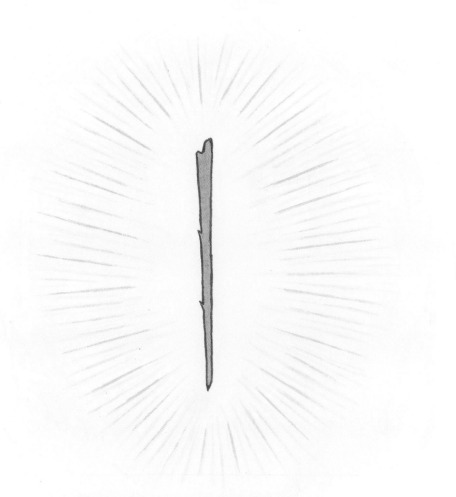

He knew at last he had
found his voice.

But for now, the stick didn't want
to get wet.

So he took a fallen leaf and made
himself an umbrella.

For he truly was
a clever stick.

But the stick didn't care. He
knew he could make another.

The animals scattered, the plants closed their leaves, and within minutes the stick's masterpiece was washed away.